This Little Tiger book
belongs to:

_____

_____

_____

For Torben, with love
~ M C B

To Jack Aldridge Palmer
~ T M

LITTLE TIGER PRESS LTD,
an imprint of the Little Tiger Group
1 Coda Studios,
189 Munster Road, London SW6 6AW
www.littletiger.co.uk

First published in Great Britain 2020
This edition published 2021
Text copyright © M Christina Butler 2020
Illustrations copyright © Tina Macnaughton 2020

A CIP catalogue record for this book is available from the British Library
All rights reserved • ISBN 978-1-78881-686-1
Printed in China • LTP/1800/1337/0420
10 9 8 7 6 5 4 3 2 1

One Christmas Wish

M Christina Butler • Tina Macnaughton

LITTLE TIGER

LONDON

Little Hedgehog and his friends were having tea when a flurry of snow fluttered past the window.

"It's going to be a white Christmas!"
said Rabbit excitedly.

"Yippee!" squeaked the baby mice.
"We can build snow mice!"

"Let's make them together!
Come over tomorrow, everyone,"
suggested Little Hedgehog.

But the next day, the snow had melted.
"It's all gone!" cried the baby mice.
"We can't build snow mice without snow."

"Don't give up!" replied Little Hedgehog kindly.
"Look, there's some snow on those branches
and a little under that bush. If we collect
it in my hat, we'll have enough in no time!"
"A snow hunt!" they all cheered.

"We wish you a Merry
Christmas," everyone sang
as they searched through the
woods and up Rocky Ridge, collecting
snow along the way.

When they reached the very top,
they found a blanket
of glistening snow.
"Let's make snow
angels!" laughed
Rabbit, diving in.

Busily, they all scooped the snow into Little
Hedgehog's hat, until it was full to the brim.

Then Badger declared, "Time to head back!"
and off they went.

They were halfway home when they passed
Grandpa Squirrel decorating his tree.
"Can we help?" offered Little Hedgehog.
"Oh, thank you!" smiled Grandpa Squirrel.

When the last bauble was in place, the friends stepped back to admire the tree.

"It still doesn't look very Christmassy," sighed Grandpa Squirrel. "Something's missing."

The baby mice knew exactly what it was . . .

"What a jolly Christmas
Eve this is turning into,"
smiled Little Hedgehog
as the friends set off.

"You need some snow
to frost the needles!"
they announced.
"Perfect!" beamed
Grandpa Squirrel.
"How kind you are!"

Near the riverbank, they found the Beavers looking glum.
"We planned a winter snowball fight," they explained,
"but the snow's melted!"
The baby mice rushed over to the snow-filled hat.
"We have just the thing . . ." they chuckled.

"Ready, steady . . . snowball fight!" yelled
a baby mouse, throwing the first ball.
 They shared out handfuls of snow and
everyone joined in.

"Goodness!" exclaimed Rabbit,
looking up. "We'd better head
home before it gets dark."
  "Race you back!"
called Fox, bounding
off into the wood.
But Fox hadn't got
far when . . .

"OUCH!"

he tripped and landed with a bump.

"Oh dear, that foot does look sore," said
Badger, taking a closer look. "But nothing
a cold compress can't fix!"

"We can use our snow!" chorused
the baby mice.

With the hat fastened round Fox's
foot, and Badger and Rabbit
by his side, the friends
walked slowly back to
Little Hedgehog's
house.

"Time for cocoa!" said Badger
when they arrived.

"And we can build our snow mice!"
giggled the baby mice. But when they
peeked inside Little Hedgehog's hat . . .

. . . the very last flake was melting
at the bottom!

"The snow!" everyone gasped.

"It's all gone!"

"Christmas won't be special
without it," cried the baby mice.
Mouse hugged them close.
"You've already made
Christmas special," she said,
"by sharing your snow."

"Our snow did bring lots of happiness,"
they sniffed.
    "And Christmas isn't over yet!" added
Little Hedgehog, waving goodbye.
"Come back tomorrow and we'll
all celebrate together!"

That evening, Little Hedgehog thought about the baby mice.

"They were so kind to give away their snow," he sighed. "There must be a way to make their Christmas wish come true."

Suddenly he had an idea.

All through the night he painted and glued . . .

folded and snipped, until his
surprise was finally ready.

On Christmas Day, Little Hedgehog's house was a wonderland of pine cones and sparkling snowflakes.

"Thank you! It's magical!" marvelled the baby mice. "But there's something even MORE magical . . ."

"What's that?" smiled Little Hedgehog.

"Spending Christmas with all our friends!" they laughed, as fresh flakes of snow fluttered past the window.

More fantastically festive stories from Little Tiger . . .

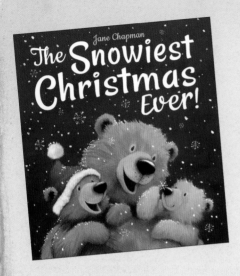

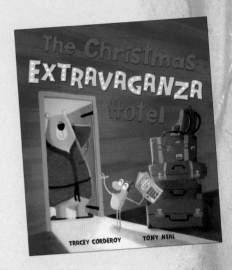

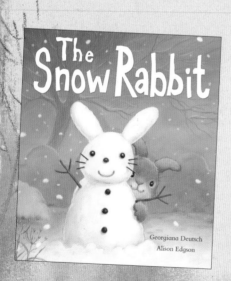

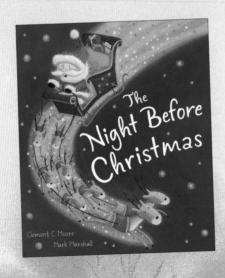

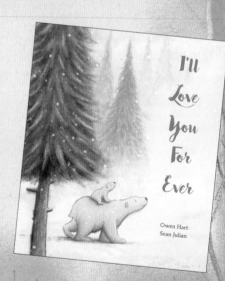

 LITTLE TIGER

For information regarding any of the above titles
or for our catalogue, please contact us:
Little Tiger Press Ltd, 1 Coda Studios, 189 Munster Road,
London SW6 6AW • Tel: 020 7385 6333
E-mail: contact@littletiger.co.uk • www.littletiger.co.uk